This book is dedicated to my loving family —
I cherish and love you to the moon and back.

To my other family, my farm team —
For loving and caring for my animals, and for having an endless
amount of patience with me.

To Laura Jesseph and the Love GOGA team —
For always having my "baaa-ck."

To Hope Easter Malenke Bennett of North Georgia Wildlife Park —
For inspiring me in so many ways.

To Dr. Stewart Colby & Ben Hortman of Windward Animal Hospital —
For taking care of my furry friends.

To Dr. Stephanie Hall —
For dropping everything and coming to my rescue in farm
emergencies.

To Wendy Green of Love and Light With Purpose —
For the mentorship, love and light you always give me.

I love you all and thank you for your support in my writing this book.

Lenny & Lou's Llamazing Treasure Hunt

By Cathi Huff & Danielle Bartling

Illustrated by Bianca Clark

Lenny and Lou woke up from their nap feeling energized and refreshed. It was a beautiful sunny Sunday, and the two llama brothers were ready to play.

They needed something fun to do that would keep them out of trouble. Yesterday, Farmer Cathi mentioned that they should stay busy and productive.

Lenny and Lou trotted over to the nursery to visit the goat girls.

"Hey girls, do you want to come play on the swingset with me and Lenny?"

"Sorry, we're busy practicing yoga for our next 'Goga' session. We don't have time to play right now," the goat girls replied.

Disappointed yet determined, Lenny and Lou skipped off to visit the piglets.

Milton and Mabel were sunbathing in their sparkly blue pool eating popsicles that their Aunt Laura had bought for them the day before. Between bites, the piglets took turns blowing bubbles at Bronx and Dolly who were not amused by the silly game.

"Hey Milton! Hey Mabel! Do you want to play hide-and-seek with us?" Lenny asked the piggy siblings.

Milton and Mabel shook their heads and replied, "No thanks. We want to stay nice and cool in the pool."

Lenny and Lou paused for a moment and considered jumping in the water, too. But their fur was freshly shampooed and fluffed, and Farmer Cathi would not be pleased if they ruined their new blowouts.

Lenny and Lou decided to try one more time to find playmates so they stopped by the pond to chat with the goose girls.

"Hey Allie, Robyn, and Stephanie! Will you play a game of hopscotch with us? We are really bored and want something fun to do."

The geese honked loudly and replied in a serious tone, "Absolutely not! We are on duty guarding the gate and don't have time for foolish games."

Lenny and Lou hung their long necks low, almost touching the ground. They were disappointed that no one wanted to play. The heavy-hearted llamas decided to hunt for four-leaf clovers until suddenly, the thought occurred to Lenny…

"Let's create a treasure hunt with our friends' favorite things! They will simply have to play with us if they ever want to find them."

"Genius! Let's do it," replied little Lou.

The llamas snuck over to the canine apartment where the patrol dogs were sound asleep in their beds. While searching for items to snag for the hunt, Lou pointed out Charlie's favorite wishbone chewy lying next to him.

"Charlie will be so excited to find this," Lenny whispered as he slipped the wishbone into his bag.

Lou then spotted Captain Crunch's sheriff hat hanging on the wall but he couldn't reach it, not even on his tippy toes, so Lenny reached up and grabbed the hat with his teeth.

"Ooh, shiny!" Lou said as he scampered across the room.

"Let's hide Rosie and Ruby's badges, too. They will surely want to find these."

Lenny scooped up the shiny stars with the hat and tucked it all in his bag.

Their next stop was the teen goat stall where they found Lucy the Lamb snoozing and counting sheep in her sleep, "One… two…three…" she mumbled.

"FLOOR!" Lou exclaimed in a loud whisper. "Lenny, look at the floor!" Lucy's soft fleece blanket had slid off her cot and crumpled on the ground next to her.

"Are you thinking what I'm thinking?" Lenny asked coyly. The llamas smiled at each other, then Lenny scooped up the blanket and tucked it into his bag.

As they exited the barn, Lenny and Lou spied the goose girls who were still on duty at the gate. The llamas tiptoed quietly behind them to avoid being seen.

"Ooh, even shinier!" exclaimed Lou at the sight of three golden necklaces.

"Shhh," Lenny whispered. "If they hear us, they'll wake everyone up with their loud honks. Let's grab and go." He snagged the diamond necklaces and carefully placed them in the zippered pocket of his bag.

Finally, it was time to hide the treasures. The llamas ran up the grassy hill to find their first hiding spot — a patch of dirt where Charlie likes to bury his toys.

Lou dug a hole with his little hooves, and Lenny planted Charlie's wishbone inside. They patted down dirt to seal the hole and staked a tiny makeshift sign to mark the spot.

"High hoove!" The llamas cheered and high-fived as best as they could.

Lenny and Lou galloped to the opposite end of the pasture where Lucy often sunbathes. Once again, Lou dug the hole and Lenny buried the blanket.

"Teamwork makes the dream work!" Lou piped proudly.

Lenny agreed, "Everyone will be playing with us in no time."

Their next stop was the sandbox on the pond's shoreline.
Lou dug another hole, Lenny buried the goose girls'
necklaces deep in the sand, and they planted another sign.

The llamas were growing tired from all the running and digging, but they were determined to finish the game. They inhaled, exhaled, and continued on their way.

Hopping along the fence line to Grandma Geraldines's house, Lou's little legs were exhausted, but he managed to dig one more hole for Lenny to hide the sheriff's hat and badges. Moments after planting the sign, they heard rustling in the barn.

"Yippee! I think our playmates are waking up," cheered Lou.

"Perfect timing," said Lenny with a mischievous smile.

Over at the barn, the dogs were indeed waking up from their naps. Captain Crunch felt around in his pocket for the heart-shaped necklace he had given Max the Pig before he passed away. Lo and behold – the necklace was gone! Captain turned his pocket inside out and discovered a small tear in the fabric.

"Woof! Code red... Max's necklace is missing," announced the worried Captain.

Ruby and Rosie's sleepy eyes shot open, and they hastily rolled over to reach for their badges on the shelf.

"Oh no!" Ruby shouted. "Our badges are missing too!"

With his eyes still closed, Charlie took a single sniff and noticed right away that his wishbone was no longer next to him.

"Awooooo! Who took my favorite chewy?" Charlie wailed.

In the stall next door, Charlie's howling had woken Lucy up. She felt a chilly afternoon breeze and reached for her favorite blanket, but that was gone, too.

Lucy shouted, "Hey, did someone borrow my blanket? I'm freezing!"

Across the pond, the geese had finished guard duty for the day and waddled back to their house to get gussied up for a party later. Stephanie opened the jewelry box and noticed all three necklaces missing. The girls were shocked as they had been on duty all day, and they knew for a fact no intruders had breached the gate.

"HONK! Who took our jewelry!?" Stephanie yelled.
"HONK! How could this happen!?" Allie screeched.
"HONK! What do we do!?" Robyn panicked.

All the animals gathered in a frenzy, frantically asking each other if they had seen their beloved items. While the chaos erupted inside and outside the barn, Lenny and Lou were lounging lazily on their backs, resting after their mission. Lenny casually stood up and announced with a grin, "We might know where your things are... Do you want to go on a treasure hunt with us?"

The animals looked puzzled at first, but then they looked angry.

Captain Crunch addressed Lenny and Lou with authority, "Did you steal our favorite things?"

"Ha! No, we didn't steal them. It's a game," Lou replied cheekily. "Who wants to play?"

The dogs huffed and puffed. The geese and goat girls rolled their eyes. Lucy let out a long-winded sigh.

"Follow us. Let's have some fun," Lenny said with a wink.

Frustrated but determined to find their favorite things, the animals obliged the eager llamas.

Lenny and Lou led the way followed by Captain Crunch, Rosie, Ruby, Charlie, Lucy, the piglets, the geese, and the goat girls trailing reluctantly behind. Their first stop was Charlie's hiding spot. He didn't need a sign to tell him where to look — he smelled his wishbone right away and dug as fast as his paws would go until he found it.

"Yippee!" Charlie cheered. "My most favorite toy in the whole world!" Then he started munching on it.

Lenny and Lou then skipped over to the sandbox and instructed everyone to keep up. The goose girls were the first to spot their sign.

Stephanie, Allie, and Robyn dug their beaks in the sand over and over again until they retrieved each golden necklace. The geese honked three big sighs of relief and secured the jewelry around their long necks.

A few feet away, Lucy spotted a sign marked with black and white polka dots. She immediately recognized the pattern and began kicking up the earth with her hooves. Lucy spotted a corner of her blanket, grabbed it with her teeth, and yanked it out of the ground. Then, she wrapped herself in it like a burrito.

The patrol dogs grew frustrated and asked, "What about our stuff?" Captain Crunch zeroed in on Lenny with a stern look since he's the older llama brother.

"Just one more stop!" Lenny said as he led everyone to the fence. Upon spotting their sign, the dogs dug using their massive paws until their hidden treasures were revealed.

Captain brushed the dirt off his hat and placed it on his head. Ruby and Rosie blew the dust off their badges and pinned them on.

"Wait. Hold your horses!" Captain boomed. "Where's Max's necklace?"

The llamas blinked at each other in confusion. Captain Crunch dragged his paw over the hole in his pocket and gently wiped a tear from his eye.

"Don't look at us!" Lenny said, visibly puzzled. "That wasn't part of our plan."

"I promise we didn't—" Lou began but was interrupted by a sudden burst of high-pitched chirping sounds.

The animals darted their eyes in different directions to identify what or who it was.

"Hello? Who's there?" Lenny asked, just as confused as everyone else.

Suddenly, a small flock of fluffy chicks appeared, popping their heads out from behind the bushes and giggling. One by one, inch by inch, they marched over to a mysterious, smaller sign with a heart scratched onto it.

"Dig! Dig! Dig!" peeped the cheerful baby chickens, jumping up and down.

Captain took the order to heart. He ran over to the sign and dug his paws into the ground. He kept digging until he uncovered a velvet, gem-engraved treasure box. The animals circled around him as he opened it. Inside was the missing heart necklace along with a tiny note that read, "Love is all you need."

As it turns out, earlier in the day, the chicks had found the gold heart necklace in the grass near their coop. It had fallen out of Captain's pocket and they wanted to return it to him. They knew how special the necklace was to everyone since it was a reminder of their angel pig, Max.

Lenny realized his treasure hunt was more than just a fun game, it was about bringing the animals together. Everyone was relieved to have found their favorite things but most of all, they were grateful for time spent with each other because…

Love really is

all you need.

In real life, Lenny and Lou are two mischievous best friends and llama brothers who enjoy stirring up trouble at Atlantis Dream Farm – but all in good fun!

P.S. There's a treasure hunt for you, too! The chicks hid their eggs on each page. How many can you find?